BEASTLY FEASTS!

A Mischievous Menagerie in Rhyme

ROBERT L. FORBES

Drawings by Ronald Searle

Overlook Duckworth

New York · Woodstock · London

First Edition
First published in the United States in 2007 by
Overlook Duckworth, Peter Mayer Publishers, Inc.
New York, Woodstock, and London

NEW YORK:
141 Wooster Street
New York, NY 10012

WOODSTOCK:
One Overlook Drive
Woodstock, NY 12498
www.overlookpress.com
[For individual orders, bulk and special sales, contact our Woodstock office]

LONDON:
Gerald Duckworth & Co. Ltd.
Greenhill House
90-93 Cowcross Street
London EC1M 6BF

Text has been set in ITC Berekley Old Style, Khaki, and hand lettered initials by Ronald Searle.

Cataloging-in-Publication Data is available from the Library of Congress.

Book design and type formatting by Bernard Schleifer
Manufactured in China
3 5 7 9 8 6 4 2
ISBN 10: 1-58567-929-1
ISBN 13: 978-1-58567-929-4

For Lydia, my Wife,

My Dance Partner in Life

CONTENTS

BEASTLY FEASTS!

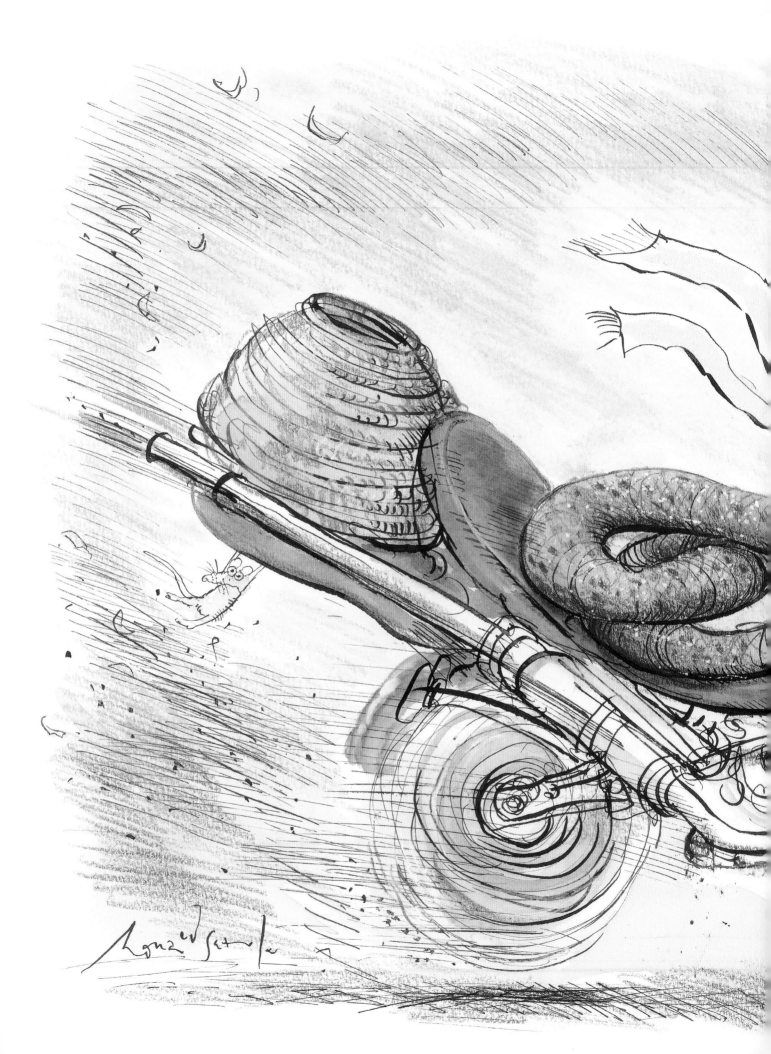

SPIKE THE BIKER

I once knew a cobra named Spike
Who lived in a round wicker basket.
He rode a loud-sounding bike,
But the cheap gas he bought blew a gasket.
So he crashed going fast down the pike
And came home in a long wicker casket.

THE RHINOSAURUS

When you feel the earth shake, at the drive-through zoo,
Better take a look around, he might be after you.
Not only is he enormous, he's also very fast –
He is the Rhinosaurus, a beastie from the past.

(Some grown-ups use a different name, insisting on Rhinoceros,
But you'll agree it's not quite right; for us, it's way too serious.)

You must pay careful attention, because he'll cleverly hide
By a bush – then WHAM! – a push! Your car is on its side!
He pokes his horn to pull you out and chase you all around,
And with a BAM! – he stomps the ground to make sure you fall down.

He picks you up then by your belt to toss you in the air!
When you descend, avoid his horn; it hurts to land right there.
It's fun to sit upon his back but Rhino hates a rider,
So he'll bounce to get you off, though soon gets tired and tired-er!

Quick! Slide off! Now run back home and snuggle into bed,
And let me read you stories, my precious sleepyhead.
But wait! That rumble! Oh my goodness! Look who's coming
        towards us!
He's back! He's mad! He's got you now! The beastie Rhinosaurus!

THE HAPPY KANGAROO

See the happy kangaroo
With her little baby-boo
Who rides the pouch on her tummy
And snuggles happy next to mummy.
When he's bigger he can play
Outside her pouch with pals all day.
He learns to hop alongside Ma,
Taking big-boy leaps like Pa.
Older yet, he shows kid brother
The jumping tricks he learned from mother.
Soon he looks for girls to date
And, like his chums, then woos a mate.
That's the way life goes with kangaroos
And all their little baby-boos.

THE CHITTERY-CHATTERY CRAB

A crab I know named Ahab
Is a clickety-clack chatter-box
Who for hours will yap and blab
To his pals in the pools on the rocks.

The sea tales he tells these hard-shelled friends
In his chittery-chattery way
Have beginnings but cleverly never have ends,
To make sure they'll be back every day.

On the ins and outs of the tide
He'll skitter, but all of a sudden
He stops and stomps his legs on one side
To show off the two that are wooden!

His yarns have a crusty, saltwater appeal –
On and on he goes, yakkety-yak,
Our hero from crow's nest to keel,
As he ships 'round the world and back.

Old Ahab's chatter starts to sputter
With the rays of the sea-setting sun,
And when his scootle becomes a slow scutter,
This ancient mariner's day is done.

BITTY AND BOBBY

Bitty the Bedbug bit Bobby the Bat
While he was tucked into his bed.
But he sleeps upside down
So she got turned around
And instead of his toe bit his head.

HARRY THE LAZY RABBIT

Harry was a lazy guy, a quite peculiar rabbit,
Who liked to lounge around, a dangerous bad habit.
Any chance he found to nap, he'd grab it!
He'd sneak to the garden for lettuce and nab it,
But then he'd curl up – he just couldn't stop.
Even at carrot cake parties, down he'd flop.
Harry's story ends with the last garden crop
Which was doggedly guarded by a tough canine cop
Who caught Harry resting and chewed him to bits –
Proving the truth that not everything fits
The usual rules, like poor Harry's unnatural habit
Of being a snoozeful, un-hoppy rabbit.

THE LOCAL GNUS

You say you know too little about gnus?
Then here's a tour that should amuse
By giving you a few close-up views
Of what they do at the Club Zoo de Gnus.
There gnu members pay hefty dues,
And ladies always do teas in twos,
With fine tea cups in hues of blues.
Oooh what posh pastries they choose
While they chew over recent gnu news,
Like who's got the latest sniffle-y flus
Or who saw whom on the singles cruise.
In the Grill the gents savor a stew
Of whatever the chef just slew,
With potatoes mashed by his crew,
All washed down with Gnuweiser, the club's own brew,
And then it's time for an armchair snooze.

Now, aren't you glad you didn't lose
This chance to know your local gnus?

THE TORTFUL TORTOISE

Tommy the Tortoise, a lawyer I know,
Is a regular ambulance chaser.
He's very well suited and puts on a show,
For he's also a marathon racer.

He serves up subpoenas and tortuous torts
In his running pursuit of more money.
He thinks he's tough when he harrumphs and snorts,
And he doesn't find lawyer jokes funny.

PANTHER CAKES

Babu the panther, whose passion is cooking,
Relies on instinct, spending little time looking
Through recipes and instead piles on spices
While mixing and chopping with his kitchen devices
The signature dish he calls Panther Cakes.
He puts on his apron, and to begin he takes
The easiest possible ingredients to find
And begins to slice and sliver and grind
Them into pieces to throw in the pot.
Babu doesn't care if they're fat or not,
Or tall or small or mealy or lean.
He knows exactly what they've done to be mean
To a sister or parent or dog or young brother,
And if they are sorry, he'll just find another
Rascal to serve to panthers worldwide
In thick, tender panther cakes, juicily fast fried,
No extra fillers, like day-old bread crumbs,
Just bad boy bits. He works as he hums,
"Such fine Panther Cakes, by chef Babu.
The choicest of bullies, cooked up for you!"

THE CONSERVATIVE LOBSTER

A conservative lobster was friend Ned
Who quite believed: better dead than Red.
"Ironic is it not," as he slid into the pot,
Said Ned, "I end up red when I am dead."

THE BOAR AT MY DOOR

There was a boar
Outside my door.
I opened wide.
He ran inside.
He cursed and swore
And swore some more.
He was furious!
I was curious.
Around his tusk
A bagel crust –
He shook his head
'Til he turned red.
To and fro,
It would not go!
I said, "Wait!
It's not too late."
Then my wife
Gave me a knife.
I cut it free.
He said to me,
"With my snuffle
I'll find a truffle.
You'll eat well."
I said, "Swell!"
Off he went,
This bristled gent,
To find the kid
Who now was hid,
Whose wicked trick
Had been to stick
On his tusk
That bagel crust.

WINSTON'S DINNER

I once knew an owl named Winston
Who loved a main course of mice,
And for dinner he always would mince one
In a stew with carrots and rice.

But as he got older and wiser,
For meals no more mice would he hurt.
The mice thought it nice, but it would be nicer
If he'd then skip the mousie dessert!

THE LOG WITH BUMPS

The alligator swims around,
But mostly he does not.
He lies there like a log with bumps,
And dreams of treats he eats a lot –

Like kids or fluffy dogs that bark,
The golfer who's lost a ball.
Yet hear his heartfelt thanks at dark,
He's not a handbag at the mall.

So keep your poochie by your side,
And leave the golf ball where it hid;
Moms and dads must fast decide
Who's to mind the squirmy kid,

For oh how quick he wanders off
In search of pranks or worse.
The 'gator finds him tender, soft –
The sweet revenge of next year's purse!

HAPLESS NAPLESS GEORGE

A pelican I know once had a cousin George
Whose mom said to him, "Dear, you're young and need your daily nap.
I know you'd rather go and fish
To fill your bill with a seafood dish;
It's risky business when you gorge,
'Cause when you're tired you hit the sea with such an *awful* slap."

But every day he'd sneak away on his glutton's flight,
'Til one afternoon he plain forgot and fished and fished as day turned dark.
Tired out, his plunges turned erratic,
His success ever more sporadic,
When – too late! – he realized his mom was right:
His noisy dives were a dinner bell for hungry mister shark.

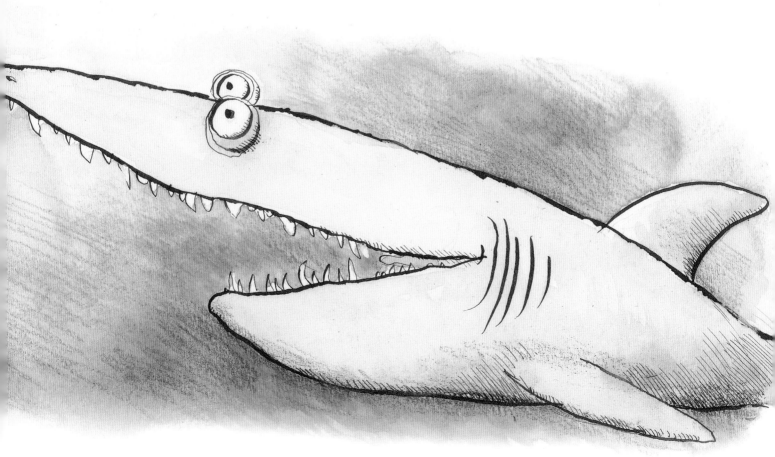

THE GINGER TUB TABBY

I said to the Ginger Tub Tabby,
Do you want to get so flabby
From eating lots of ginger fish pies?
He cries,
Me-oww-my, but I *loves*
Them ginger fish pies.

So I said to the Ginger Tub Tabby,
Then be happy and get a bit flabby
From eating your ginger fish pies.
He sighs,
Me-oww-my, I so *loves*
Them ginger fish pies.

LOTTIE THE HOTTIE

An uptown leopard named Lottie
All the guys consider a hottie.
They vie to make the night scene
With this dazzling prowl-and-growl queen,
While the papers send top paparazzi
For shots of our cool hotsy-totsy –
No predator photographs better
At the kill than this jungle trendsetter,
Decked out not in regular spots
But in bright black-and-white polka dots.

OLD SLOTHY

A gentleman, my friend, the sloth.
He doesn't *do*; rather, he doth.
And when he moveth, as such,
It's only thither and not very much.

BEARSNEEZE

I knew a boy who had a cold but snuck off to the zoo.
There he dashed to feed the bear.
Take care! You'll catch your death – Ah-choo!
A naughty lad, he took no care and in the end did feed the bear –
An accident. A flu-ful chew.
That's how bruin caught a cold –
Ah-choo, ah-CHOO, AH-CHOO!

A PECULIAR PAIR

The early bird and the night owl
Are a peculiar pair.
It may seem odd their marriage works
Since both are rarely there.

His nocturnal job is catching food
Until the dark's near gone.
Done, he swoops his way back home
On rosy rays of dawn.

So he tugs his jammies on
And trundles into bed,
Just as she is getting up
To plan the day ahead.

She catches worms to feed the kids
And sends them off to school,
Then dusts and cleans and mops and mends
Until the evening's cool.

He wakes anew and joins her in
Twilight's softening hour.
They talk and listen, sharing thoughts,
Snug in their treetop bower.

Then he's away and she's to bed:
I wonder, please, now you've heard –
Aren't they peculiar, as I said,
The night owl and the early bird?

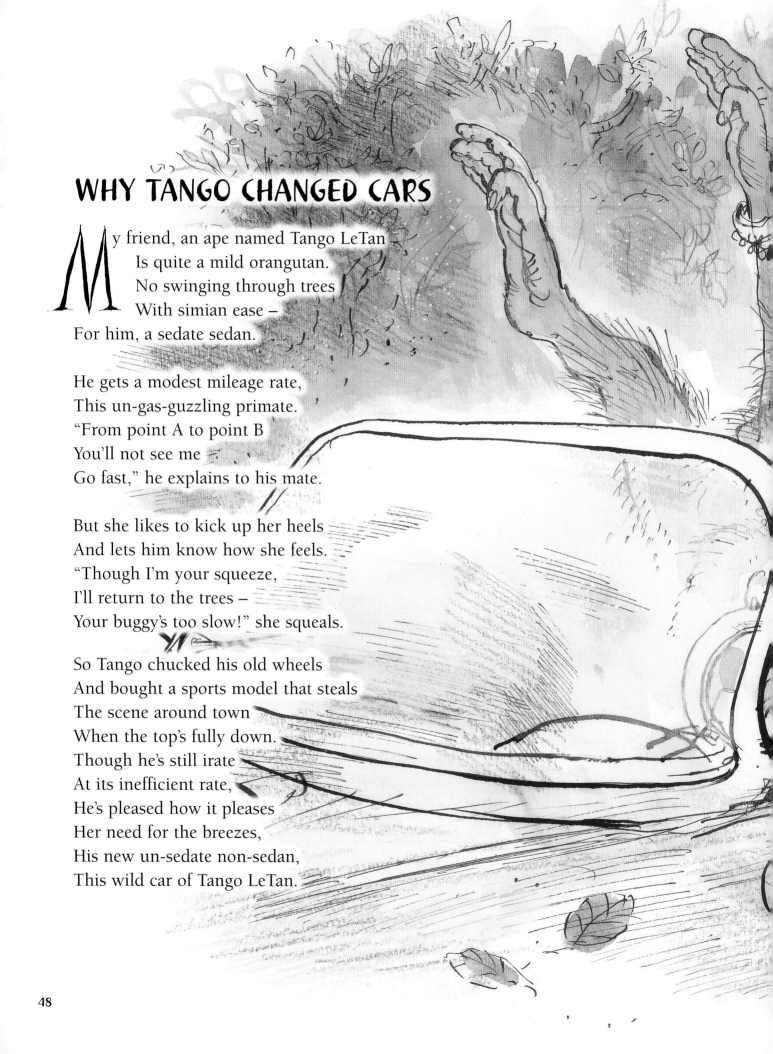

WHY TANGO CHANGED CARS

My friend, an ape named Tango LeTan
Is quite a mild orangutan.
No swinging through trees
With simian ease –
For him, a sedate sedan.

He gets a modest mileage rate,
This un-gas-guzzling primate.
"From point A to point B
You'll not see me
Go fast," he explains to his mate.

But she likes to kick up her heels
And lets him know how she feels.
"Though I'm your squeeze,
I'll return to the trees –
Your buggy's too slow!" she squeals.

So Tango chucked his old wheels
And bought a sports model that steals
The scene around town
When the top's fully down.
Though he's still irate
At its inefficient rate,
He's pleased how it pleases
Her need for the breezes,
His new un-sedate non-sedan,
This wild car of Tango LeTan.

ODE ON A FISHBOWL

The goldfish swims in swift gyration,
Living to be fed
His fish food, not to be food,
For someone wants him dead.
His life is just a big bowl
And nowhere can he hide;
With glass and water all around,
He's always magnified.
He looks out from his thin weeds
And sees what he most fears:
Two big eyes, and whiskers,
And pointy little ears,
Plus teeth, and tongue that slowly licks
Pink lips that when they part,
Reveal the horrifying abyss
Which leads to kitty's heart of dark.

In that bowl, what kitty sees
Riles and tries his patience,
For long ago his ancestors

Were worshipped by the ancients
Who honored kitty as a god,
Like Sphinx upon the Nile.
But now he gets so little respect,
His cat life is a trial.
Glittery, golden, looming large,
Fish loves to mock poor kitty
With a toothy fin-face grin,
And here's the final pity:
For though his foe would taste sublime,
The fishy world is wet.
Since kitty's greatest dread is water,
All he can do is be a threat.

So life's a standoff, each side caught
In their mutual trance,
Frozen, fearing, taunted, teasing,
Waiting for the chance
To break the spell, to find release
From their eternal dance.

THE UNFLUTTERY BUTTERFLY

A butterfly I know finds it hard to flutter,
Eating no margarine, preferring only real butter.
She heaps thick cream and jam on her scones
And just can't resist cherry-vanilla cones.
Such a dairy-rich diet high in cholesterolics
Of course gums up her flying hydraulics.
The consequence of her excessive pounds
Is that it's hard to make her rounds,
But the butter intensifies her iridescence
To a rainbowy glow of incandescence.

While flying is no longer this gal's thing,
She still can wiggle a come-hither wing,
Enough to attract guys who desperately seek
A nod or a wink or a kiss on the cheek
By bringing her treats that are so utterly
Conducive to a life now lived un-flutterly.

THE BALLAD OF EARL THE SQUIRREL

There once was a show-offy squirrel
Who had changed his name to Earl,
(It used to be Sid when he was a kid)
And, yes, his girl was named Pearl.

Now Earl worked out with weights
And took Pearl out on dates
Where he wore flashy duds and drank mugs of suds –
Just the boyfriend mom squirrel hates.

Hanging out at the park every day
To hustle his food and not pay,
He'd stake out a bunch of kids with their lunch
To attack them and steal it away.

Squirrels are notoriously rude,
As they shamelessly beg for your food,
But Earl felt superior and thought them inferior
To him, a most righteous dude.

Along came a bright boy named Joe
Who figured out what he needed to know
To outsmart the pest who bothered the rest
By pinching their food on the go.

So to Earl he offered a deal:
"Stick with me and I'll bring you a daily meal
You'll happily swallow, and then get to wallow
In snacks you won't have to steal."

Oh bliss! Oh joy! What a gig!
Joe's servings were supersized big.
But Earl didn't know that he'd started to show
What happens when you eat like a pig.

One night he waddled back to his home base,
Where he knew his girl Pearl he would face.
He came to their tree but then found that he
Was too heavy to climb! Oh disgrace!

He fell down and started to cry,
And wailed, "Gosh, why didn't I
See that my figure was unnaturally bigger
Once I gave up food on the fly?"

His sobbings soon perked up the ears
Of the one foe every squirrel fears:
It's Old Al the cat who grinned knowing that
These were Earl's last tears.

The next day all they could find
Was what poor Earl left behind:
His torn sequined suit that had been such a hoot,
Though Pearl, coolly, paid it no mind.

For she'd grown disgusted with Earl,
No longer her grooviest squirrel.
He wound up sleazy when life got too easy –
"Oh, what a swine!" said Miss Pearl.

THE TIGER AND THE TYKE

Tiger, tiger, fearsome sight,
Giving little brother fright.
The older brat scoffs, "It's a fraud,
There's a cage – we can't be clawed!"

Tiger, tiger, pacing fast,
His snarling leaves the tot aghast.
Big brother sneers at the big cat's rage,
For strong steel bars do make that cage.

Tiger, tiger, there you are –
Don't you see your door ajar?
Careless keepers did the deed,
Distracted when they brought your feed.

Tiger, tiger, out the gate,
Tiger will not hesitate,
To slash a mortal's hand or eye –
Pray, who will be the first to die?

Tiger, tiger, pounces fast
To grab a kid who'll breathe his last.
I wish tiger had clawed the other,
But the older boy outran his brother.

HIPPO UH-OH!

There's a hippo that I know,
Who's always snacking on the go.
He eats 'til he's about to bust,
And then the hippo potty must!

PRINCE VINCE

There was a dachshund Prince,
An arrogant pup named Vince
Whose Kingly Dad, Vince Senior,
Was appalled at Junior's demeanor.
He said, "Son, as royalty,
You must inspire loyalty
From all the dogs in the town
Who vow allegiance to our crown."
But Vince felt a daily bone
Was the tax owed to the throne.
They piled up, and each dawn
He buried them in the Great Lawn.

When Vince Senior passed away
His heir declared it was the day
To raise the price of the tribute,
But resentment was taking deep root,
As subjects began to growl and say,
"If our new King has his way,
All our bones will go to him
Leaving our cupboards thinly grim."
They revolted and Vince lost his job,
To the delight of the baying mob,
And once Bad Vince was dethroned
The Great Lawn of the Palace was deboned.
He was left with a grubby dirt hole
And a meager daily dog-food bowl.
He'd been mean, but now life is meaner
For Vince, the once Princely Weiner.

LEON THE CHAMELEON

I know a bright chameleon named Leon,
An aspiring actor whose name in neon
Lights he wanted, but when he went on
The set they had to put too much makeup on
Him since his natural camouflage came on,
And so he quit and decided on
A detective career so he can spy on
Everyone and they won't see him sneak up on
Them. And so it goes, eon after eon:
Chameleons learn they must blend in, like Leon.

OLD COMPLAINFUL

Sam the Ram finds everything's wrong.
That's why he's called Old Complainful.
With his "ifs" and "ands" he can be headstrong,
But it's the "buts" of Old Complainful that are painful.

THE HEAD BEE BUSTER

I knew a Head Bee named Buster,
Who buzzed through the hive with bluster.
In the spring flower bed he'd stick in his head
And zip away with a pollen-ful luster.

Said the Queen one day, My dear Buster,
I demand all the pollen you can muster.
But he had to roam too far from home
And was gassed by a passing crop duster.

The Queen quickly found without Buster
That the drive in the hive grew lackluster.
Her Majesty's need had pushed her to greed
And left her in a worried buzz-fluster.

The hive slowly dried and went bust
For this Queen had lost her swarm's trust.
She got on her knees and said, Don't go, please!
But they all fled and the hive turned to dust.

THE DEBONAIR FOX

A friend, a debonair fox,
Is fashionable down to his socks.
When chased by the hounds on a tour of the grounds,
It's their ill-bred habits he mocks.

There's a hunt dog returned in a box,
Having died on the rainy-slick rocks:
"Isn't it swell he's turned in his wellies,
Poor mutt!" mocks our debonair fox.

NATHANIEL NEWT

Nathaniel Newt was crossing the road,
    Fulfilling his destiny's dream
Of kick-starting life by getting to water
    And finding the sun's warming beam;
But crossing the road is a risk-fraught quest:
    Nature's roulette, it would seem –
For poor Nat got squished by a car full of kids
    On their way to play in his stream.

GORELLICK GORILLA

Gorellick Gorilla, King of the Myth, said, "I'm not a herbivore.
Don't like roots; can't stand shoots! In fact, I'm a carnivore.
So bring me a pigmy, yummy-bite-size for big me,
And the jungle will be peaceful once more."

STRIKING STRIPES

A zebra I know named Monique
Boasts her stripes are chic-ly unique.
While other zebras' stripes go round,
Hers are straight, not up and down,
So when she roams about the veldt
Her parallel stripes are unparalleled.

COLONEL FLEMING

What Fleming learned at lemming school was always follow orders
To keep on marching, come what may, straight over the sea-cliff borders.

One day thought he, "Hey, this is dumb!" and promptly changed direction;
Those lemmings marching after him joined his insurrection.

He headed home, assuming command as their contrarian colonel,
And for a season the lemmings ceased heeding that cliff-call eternal.

But, alas, it wasn't to last, as soon a nostalgic lemming
Left the pathway for the old way, away from Colonel Fleming.

To the edge and then right on over went a massive troop!
The lesson here is sadly clear
And those lemmings paid a price most dear –
Use your own mind, don't blindly follow a leader or a group!

DIZZY LIZZIE

A giraffe I know, my friend Lizzie,
Also has the nickname Dizzy.

Her neck is very, very tall,
So tall she towers o'er us all.

She's so tall it makes her proud,
For only she can eat a cloud.

WHY THE SHERIFF IS MAD

There's a tough armadillo in Texas
Who goes by the nickname of Rex as
He's the town's top gun, who vexes
All the outlaws: he's the sheriff.

He's the judge as well as the jury,
And always in a mean-headed hurry
To give you real cause to worry
About that neck of yours you cherish.

So beware! In that dusty community
Rex will take the least opportunity
To seize you with speed and impunity.
But why is this fellow so vicious?

His temper flares like a flame –
It's his parents who bear the blame
For giving him his hated name:
Just *never* call him Aloysius.

BATHTUB ADMIRAL DUANE

I know a hedgehog named Duane
Who adores a day full of rain
And digs his hole in a puddle –
Oh what a wet muddy muddle!
So he climbs in the bath with his fleet
Of warships keen to compete,
Guns firing, boom! Boom! BOOM!
As his tub floats room to room,
The flotilla at his command,
Fine vessels all, small and grand.

Hail the hero of the Ocean Navy,
Fighting battles on seas so wavy,
Finding triumph and victory
And his place in hedgehog history
As he navigates around the world,
His battle banners fully unfurled,
Courageously settling righteous scores
Off far foreign piratical shores –
Sail on! Sail on, through mud and rain,
Dear brave Bathtub Admiral Duane!

THE RACE OF THE ANTEATERS

The anteater is not a cheater;
He raced his wife and really beat her,
Arriving first, by a nose
Which, you know, is like a hose,
So he won by quite a lot!
And here is what his winning got:
On the hill he'd earned the chance
To do his special victory dance
Which stirs up lots and lots of ants.

Though she's faster – and much smarter –
She pretends she's a slow, slow starter.
That's the way he wins, it seems:
She lets them share both ants and dreams.

So every day it's ready-set-go!
He runs fast, she runs slow,
And she smiles to see his dance,
Her brave hunter of the ants.

UN-FUSSY GUSSIE

A lizard I know named Gussie
Has habits you wouldn't call fussy.
After eating she won't use a toothpick
And refuses to pick up a loose stick
To dig out the gooey bug bits,
Like wings wedged in with snug fits
Between her teeth and won't come loose
With slithering tongue or saliva juice.
She'd never ever consider a brush
Or puddle water to slursh and flush
The pieces, preferring instead to gloss
Over the mess rather than floss.

It's all so dental intensive,
A job far too labor extensive –
She figures the stuff will just rot,
And that solves the problem, does it not?

THIS WAY TO THE EGRESS

"Would you mind
To be so kind
And tell me about
The best way out?"
Said the egret.
"With regret
I find
I cannot find
The access
To the egress."
"Fine," I said,
"Straight ahead,
To the fork
By the stork.
Take a left
At that cleft,
Go round the turn
By the tern,
Then down the way
To the jay,
And through the hollow
With the swallow,
Across the plain
Where nests the crane.
As it gets dark
You'll hear the lark,
Then follow the route
Where owls hoot.
And one last left, all right?"
"Left, right?"
"Right. Left.
I hope you find
What's on your mind,
The access to the egress."
"Right!" he said,
And turned his head
In a flurry and feathery hurry,
And left.